D0516495

Weekly Reader Children's Book Club *presents*

Runaway Camel

by Ruth P. Collins

Illustrated by Harold Berson

CROWN PUBLISHERS, INC., NEW YORK

Also by Ruth P. Collins

Krishna and the White Elephant
Flying Cow
World of Curries

Library of Congress Catalog Card Number: 68–26801
Printed in the United States of America

Weekly Reader Children's Book Club Edition
Intermediate Division

"The true desert man loves his camel more than life."
—from the Koran

RUNAWAY CAMEL takes place today, in a small village in the Sahara Desert. In northern Nigeria, near Kano, one of the world's busy international airports, the great grass heights which pasture immense herds of cattle begin to change into sandy soil and gently ease off north into the desert. While highways cross the Sahara and daily flights stop at Kano, there are still many hundreds of tiny villages in the desert, little oases where the villagers live as they have for centuries. They still carry on such ancient arts as pottery, weaving, and jewelry making. Distances here are measured by the day's journey. On the caravan, pack camels go only ten or fifteen miles a day, since the camel drivers often plod on foot, with goats straggling alongside. A racing camel, however, may go 100 miles a day.

Hausa is the language spoken by most Africans in this area, and in this story the boy Musa is a member of a Hausa tribe living in an oasis about seven days' journey from Kano. For a better understanding of some of the phrases used in this story, read the Glossary in the back of the book.

CHAPTER ONE

"WATER BOY! Water boy! Musa!"

Musa, who had been sleeping on the ground outside the old mud-brick house, wakened with a start. He could hear the uproar at the village well, and now here was his grandmother coming through the gate.

The old woman hobbled up through her gourd patch and banged her empty pot down before him. "So, lazy one, you still sleep with the sun already up. And the camels and goats all trampling each other in an empty trough. And the women crying, 'No water, no water again today!' The men cursing because the ditches through the date groves have been dry these two days. Alas, alas, I knew this was going to happen again when that black feather dropped at my feet from the skies this morning."

Musa scrambled to his feet. He twisted his old scarf about his head. The usually happy face of the thirteen-year-old Hausa boy was clouded as he paused to look again toward the desert.

Grandmother spoke more gently. "Forget your camel, son. She's been gone six days now and was ailing for six months before that, turning from the fine date soup I made for her, stumbling as she turned the water-wheel."

He bit his lip, turning his face from her.

"And the people are getting cross now," she went on. "The well is left untended half the time, though there are a dozen youths waiting around to lead the camel the chief has sent down."

"And Racer. . . ." Racer was the name first given the big white camel now known to the villagers only as Lame One.

"Why, that poor old thing could not even lift her pad against a hyena," the weaver's wife joined in from over the low mud wall that separated the two yards. Musa knew that she too had heard that long, quavery *yoo-ee-ee* of a hyena last night.

Now she was putting her parrot out for his morning sun. "And I heard you too, Musa, running out there in the dark again looking for that old lame camel. Foolish boy." She held out a berry to the bird, coaxing, "Speak, pretty one, speak. Say *Allah Akbar, Allah Akbar, Allah Akbar.*" When the bird sat silent, glaring at her with red-rimmed beady eyes, she popped the berry into her own mouth and went on to Musa, "Yes, very

foolish. Did you know that Ali heard a lion out there yesterday?"

"Allah preserve us!" Grandmother hobbled over to the wall. "A lion? Why, we haven't seen a lion around this village these many years. Did you hear that, Musa? A lion!"

Musa shrugged. Ali, the camel-trader's son, always heard lions where others heard hyenas.

The weaver's wife dusted some fleece off her birdcage. It was a fine new wicker one with fancy scrolls. She had paid the basket weaver five silver coins for it. She held another berry out to the bird and coaxed again, "Say *Allah Akbar, Allah Akbar.* Yes, Ali was out looking for some of his father's camels just at sundown when he heard that awful roar behind him. He was on his way out there just now to hunt for them again when the chief sent for him to tend the well."

But at the mention of Ali's name, Musa was off down the lane. He shoved in through the noisy crowd at the well.

The waterwheel was silent. Ali, who was big for his fifteen years, was on his knees fumbling with the ropes that hitched the camel to it. All of them cried out in relief when they saw Musa, "Aha, here he is at last. Allah be praised!"

Ali shoved the ropes into Musa's hand. "Here, take your job," he said, and went galloping down the lane on his scraggy pony. Ali did not like camels. He did not like work.

Now the waterwheel was turning. Up and down the path

Musa led the chief's camel. Down splashed the big goatskin bucket into the well. And up it came to dump the cold, clear water into earthen pots, empty troughs, and ditches. Up and down it went all morning long till the old stone trough was standing full, the women all disappearing down the lane with dripping water pots on their heads, water gurgling down all the hollowed-out tree trunks that carried life to the date palms and gardens.

When the only sound that could be heard in the little village was the creaking of the waterwheel, the chief came by. The chief was the most important man in the village. He lived in a huge flat-roofed dwelling surrounded by high white walls, in the heart of the town. Once there had been armed guards at the big leather gate. But that was when the oasis had been a busy stopping place for the great caravans crossing the Sahara. Now only a bare hundred souls were left in the town and few servants in the chief's dwelling, but he still ruled as his fathers had.

A kindly, dignified old man, wearing a fine embroidered robe and turban, he sat on the side of the well and watched Musa for a time.

"You did not find the Racer yet, my son?" he called.

"No." There was a lump in Musa's throat. The chief was the only one who still called his lost camel by her proper name.

The old man shook his head, remembering. "Yes, she was

10

the fastest and noblest of all the line. You know, of course, son, that for many generations our village was known for this breed of fast white camels. Their silken fleece was used only for the scarves of chiefs. And your father was the finest rider of his day."

Musa's eyes were shining, but he still could not find words to reply.

The old man paused a moment, then went on. "It was a black day when he was lost in the great sandstorm and Racer came limping in, never to run again, but to be put to work at the waterwheel. It should never have been. She was of noble blood. Now she has died as a noble camel does, going off alone into the desert. . . ."

But Musa spoke up with spirit, "She is not dead and I know I will find her yet."

At this the chief rose and spoke sternly. "I have been very patient with you this week, water boy. The villagers are all complaining that the waterwheel is turning only half the time. I pay you five silver coins every full moon day to tend the well. And if it is left untended again, I will have to put Ali, the son of the camel trader, in your place. The camel rests only when the sun is high at noon and after it has gone down. Do you understand?"

So saying, the chief strode on down the lane.

Musa went back to the camel and began to lead it up and

down the path. The wheel began to turn. But his heart was heavy. Seeing this work camel's short stocky legs, the broad hump meant for loads, the short blunt nose pierced by a ring for the rope, he could not help thinking of his beloved Racer. Her legs were long and slender, her high hump meant only for one rider. Her long thin nose had never known a ring, for she had been trained from birth to respond to the merest whisper, the gentlest pressure of a foot on her neck. Her coat, unlike this coarse matted brown one beside him, had been soft as silk, thanks perhaps to Grandmother's bowls of date milk, and to long hours of grooming. Yes, and even while limping along the path like a work animal, she had held her head high. Sadly Musa remembered that last day.

By sundown the camel was stumbling badly, so Musa had been chanting in a high nasal voice, urging her on as the camel riders did at the end of a hard journey. He sang the song his father had sung always.

> *Swift as a bird my camel speeds,*
> *Nor wind, nor sand, nor lion heeds.*
> *Around her neck the blue stone charm*
> *To keep her safely from all harm.*
> *Lines of silver, tassels gold,*
> *A princess she of royal blood.*
> *On, on, my proud one, there ahead*
> *The well, the palm trees, and soft bed.*

But at that point Ali had come riding by and joined in the chant with a loud mocking voice. He had flipped the camel's worn noseband crying, "Oho! Lines of silver, tassels gold, eh?" When she snapped at him, for the first time in her life, he had howled in pain, *"Wai, wai, wai!* The old beast turns ugly! The chief must hear of this."

That night the camel had disappeared.

Musa looked up as a flock of goats came crowding toward the well, their small goatherd Ameena almost lost among them. Ameena was a year younger than Musa. Her father owned some of the largest flocks in the village, and like other girls she was expected to tend them out on the desert. But many a time she had taken Musa's place at the waterwheel when some duty had called him away. And while her tongue was sharp, as were all women's, her heart was kind.

Whacking with her long bamboo stick and letting out shrill cries, she came shoving through toward Musa. Her many long black pigtails and strings of gray cowrie shells were tangled, her dress rumpled, and she scolded, "Just look at the sun! And I am still chasing my goats out of the corn patches, after they all scattered at the well this morning. . . ." She broke off abruptly as she saw his face. "Listen, Musa, I have something to tell you. About your camel."

He let the rope drop and seized her arm. "Where?"

I think I saw her yesterday . . ."

"You saw her? Why didn't you tell me?"

"I couldn't find you. I looked everywhere. And," she hesitated, "I am not sure anyway. You know where the purple camel-flower grows over by the black rocks? Well, my goats strayed . . ."

"And you saw the camel?"

"No. First Ali came by on his pony. He was looking for his father's camels and I called to him to come help me, but he didn't hear—or else he was scared."

"But my camel?" Musa cried.

"I don't even know if it was a camel or not. It might have been an antelope down there in the bamboo grove. I saw only her nose, then it went bobbing off, just as the head of the Lame One bobs when she walks up and down the path here."

"And you didn't go down and get her?"

"The evil jinns . . ." she began in an awed voice.

Musa shoved the rope into her hand crying, "Here, get someone else to lead the camel," and the next moment he was racing for the desert.

He headed straight for the black rocks. Far out on the other side he could see the herds grazing. They were kept from this spot which was known to be haunted by the jinns, or evil spirits, and dangerous wild animals.

Musa had searched the spot many times this past week, and the little goat girl had not actually seen his camel, but

15

his heart was beating fast as he shoved through the waist-high camel-flower close by the bamboo grove. He began to shout, "Racer! Racer! Lame One! Lame One!" He made the familiar *g-r-r-r* sound which the camel knew.

He loved the old lame camel more than life. Six years before, when she had come limping in through a sandstorm bearing the still form of his father on her back, he had had to plead for her life. Such badly crippled animals were usually turned out on the desert to die. The villagers had shaken their heads when the chief had said, "Well, let us try her at the waterwheel."

They knew camels. Allah had made two kinds—the one to carry loads, the other messages. Racer had never known the lash, and her slender foreleg had never been tied up to keep her from wandering. Neither had she been tied nose-to-tail in the caravan. It took only an *ickth ickth* to make her kneel, or a *g-r-r-r* to send her racing. No, they all said, she would never submit to the ropes at the waterwheel.

But to everyone's surprise she had. She had stood quietly, ignoring the herds as they came jostling down the narrow lane on their way out to the desert, biting, spitting, kicking, roaring. For six years now she had plodded faithfully up and down the path, turning to nuzzle her thanks at a piece of sugarcane or a bowl of date soup Grandmother brought by.

Grandmother was always fussing over the Lame One,

16

making herb ointments for her foot, spending long hours bringing the sheen out on her coat with a bit of rough sacking. She hoarded every bit of the white fleece, which one day would go into the making of a fine scarf for a chief.

"Yes, and she was right this morning," Musa told himself as he stood now on the rock, searching for a glimpse of his camel. "The camel has been ailing these many weeks." He recalled how badly she had been breathing, how glad she was at sundown to hobble out to the desert.

Suddenly he stopped short. He had caught a glimpse of white in the bushes below. The next moment he was stumbling down over the rocks, and there before him stood Racer—looking starved, hair matted with burrs, blue stone charm dangling at the end of a broken cord, eyes wary, teeth bared. And beside her a newborn foal!

It was the tiniest camel Musa had ever seen. A ball of silky white curls wobbling on stiff knobby legs, with enormous black eyes smiling up at him.

Musa knelt for a moment to peer into the tiny fuzzy face, then jumped up and threw his arms about the neck of the old camel. He buried his face, wet with tears now, in the matted hair. "Why didn't you tell us, Racer? Who would have thought it? They said you were too old to have a foal. Or if you did, it would be a twisted ugly thing like your foot. But look at him! Look at him! Perfect!"

17

He tugged at the broken cord that held the charm, and when it was free, he knotted it and slipped it over the head of the foal. He looked back across the desert. The village was a long way off and the sun was low.

He gathered the tiny one up in his arms and started off, the Lame One following close, nose pressed to his shoulder.

CHAPTER TWO

MANY CAMELS HAD been born in the desert and carried to the little village over the years, but none had caused such a hubbub.

The whole village crowded around as Musa set the tiny camel down by the well that night. There were cries of "What a darling! What a silly little hump! See his dainty pink pads! His fluffy white curls! His lips curl up, not down—why, he laughs!"

Only Ali standing back in the shadow sneered, "Runt!"

Everyone else was happy for Musa. The little camel seemed to be laughing with them. He stood now, teetering on wobbly legs, blue stone dangling merrily, his big black eyes saying, "What happens next in this nice new world?"

"What will you name him, Musa?" someone cried out.

But before Musa could answer, the weaver's wife came

shoving through to see what was going on, and the tiny foal
caught at her string of cowrie shells, scattering them over the
ground. *"Hubba-hubba!"* she wailed.

The villagers roared with laughter. "The foal has his
name," they shouted.

Hubba-hubba meant trouble. But Musa did not care what
they called his camel. To him it was the finest ever born.

These were happy days for the water boy. As he plodded

up and down the path from the well, he sang his father's old song, dreaming of the days when once more there would be a great white racer carrying messages for the chief across the desert.

He was leading the chief's camel at the well, because the Lame One was grazing all day on the desert, as was the custom for a nursing camel. Musa knew that many camels nursed their young for as long as two years.

She kept close to the village with her foal. Musa could even see them at times, the tiny one rolling in sand, kicking up his feet, then rising on hind legs to shake his curls clean. Musa watched the foal sniff at the red cactus blossoms and run squealing to his mother when his nose was pricked. Often the little camel teased her, playing hide-and-seek around her legs, keeping out of sight of the big anxious eyes. Or again, when the wind came swirling across the sand, he would stop, head flung back, listening for a time, then go racing off screaming with joy. "He hears the jinns," Musa told himself.

Musa lived now for the hours after sundown when he would bring his camels inside the village wall. Nights he slept alongside them in the bed he had scooped from the sand. When the wind blew cold, he covered them all with his blanket or took the foal into the house.

But by the end of the first month the foal was beginning to wander. He was curious about everything. When the drivers chased him from the camels grazing far out on the sand, he made his way into the village. He trampled the baskets of fresh dates, came screaming from the fields trailing okra, yams, lentils. He sniffed at the big black pots where goat or camel meat simmered with herbs. But only once did he poke his nose into the pile of hot ashes and sand in the center of Grandmother's floor—there between great flat stones were baking the hard corn and barley cakes he liked.

He scampered through the crooked lanes, nosing into courtyards, sipping at the curds set out in the sun, splashing in the potter's clay, sniffing the dye vats. The women in the marketplace made haste to cover their wares when they saw him coming, but an hour later he was sleeping happily among them, his small sides bulging with sweets and dates. They laughed and said, *"Hubba-hubba-hubba."* He was even found nestling by the royal stool in the chief's courtyard.

Yet as the days passed Musa noticed a change. The people stopped laughing, and soon everyone was crying, *"Hubba-hubba!* Come and get this pest, water boy."

Then came the unlucky day when Hubba-Hubba managed to get into the weaver's courtyard. It was a wonderful place filled with pots of dye, mounds of camel fleece, lengths of cloth stretched out on the ground to dry, a loom from which fluttered many colored bits of yarn being turned into scarves which would be traded to passing caravans for salt. While the weaver actually wove the sturdy cloth, it was his wife who cared for all the rest.

24

The weaver's gate was kept closed because of the noisy goats and camels that jammed the lane at dawn and sundown. The weaver's wife kept a long bamboo stick close by to chase out any unlucky one that might stray in. And all day long her voice could be heard crying out to her parrot, coaxing one moment, scolding the next: "Speak, pretty one, speak. Say *Allah Akbar, Allah Akbar.*" She was determined the bird should speak before the next caravan passed by on its way to Kano, seven days' journey beyond. But so far not a sound had come from the sulky little bird.

Many times Hubba-Hubba had stood sniffing at that closed gate, wondering. And now, hearing the wails from the weaver's wife, Musa knew he had finally found his way in.

As he pushed through the laughing crowd at the gate, he saw that the weaver's wife was chasing the tiny one around the yard. In and out, clay pots crashing, dye streaming across the ground, cloth trailing, stick whacking at empty air, a merry chase was going on. It ended with Hubba-Hubba standing in the middle of the yard, framed in the loom, eyes gleaming mischievously through a tangle of colored yarn.

The weaver's wife sank down in a heap and pulled her scarf across her face, wailing, "Alas, alas, the fine new scarf my husband was weaving for the chief! And all the pots of dye I have just made for the wool. *Hubba-hubba! Hubba-hubba!*"

The crowd was murmuring *"Hubba-hubba"* too as Musa seized the tiny camel by the noseband. Then from the top of

26

the wall the parrot squawked, *"Hubba-hubba, Hubba-hubba—ha-ha-ha!"*

The weaver's wife jumped up and raced across to the wall, crying out, "You speak, pretty one. You speak at last. Speak again, pretty one. Say *Allah Akbar, Allah Akbar. . . ."*

But the parrot had drawn back into the corner of its cage and sat silent again.

Musa did not wait to hear the laugh that followed at the gate. He hustled the foal down the lane into his own yard and regarded him sadly. "Alas, alas, tiny one, what am I to do with you?"

But Hubba-Hubba merely nuzzled his soft black lips against his master's hard brown hand and began to look for more mischief. Musa led him back to a little pen behind the house, found a length of camel's-hair cord, and tied him fast to the doorpost.

After sundown when he came in from the well, he found his foal trailing a broken rope along with some of Grandmother's gourd vine. And Grandmother, old and wrinkled in a faded robe, was down on her knees wailing and peering under the leaves to see what harm had been done to her gourds.

Grandmother was known for the fine gourds she grew. Some were big enough to carry grain or even young goats to market; some were little ones used for ointments and herbs

she gathered from far out on the desert. Some she had trained by tying off a part when very young and molding them gently each day till they were grown into weird shapes. These she dried on the rooftop, then burnt in fine patterns or painted with dyes she had made from the flowers growing far out on the desert. She had her best one drying now, a huge golden jug with a long neck that flared out flower-shaped at the top. When she painted on a design, it would be ready to hold the chief's palm wine.

"Allah be praised, it's safe," Grandmother said now, looking up at Musa. "That young scamp of yours!"

"I left him tied here behind the house," Musa said. But at that moment Grandmother darted away to save the fleece she had dumped at her doorstep. It was going up in a white cloud, and all that could be seen of Hubba-Hubba was four little pads kicking high in the air.

Grandmother turned, shook a bony finger at Musa. "There's an evil spirit in that young one," she said. "Never once did his mother wander off and get into mischief like this."

Musa did not answer. He knew and so did his grandmother that the Lame One had never been left untended when young. She had been treated like a princess, groomed and fed— his father, her trainer, giving his whole time to her.

Grandmother stood looking at the foal who was up now shaking himself. Her voice softened. "Perhaps I put in too much of that herb when I mixed the date pips for the Lame

30

One. I meant only to fill the udder of the poor thing, but she still goes dry, and all the life goes into this scamp and puts mischief in his feet. I tell you, son, something must be done about him."

Musa nodded unhappily. Only that noon the chief had sent one of his servants to give the same warning. "You had better keep that foal of yours tied up, water boy," he had said. "The people in the village are beginning to say it should be destroyed."

Musa led the foal again to the back of the house, and this time he tied him to a tree trunk. Hubba-Hubba was very pleased—this rope game was something new. While Musa and the old woman stood watching, he began to tug and kick and bite, and he squealed with joy when he found himself in a hopeless tangle.

"*Hubba-hubba, hubba-hubba.* What are we to do with that animal?" Grandmother groaned.

And from the wall top nearby the parrot suddenly spoke out again, "*Hubba-hubba-hubba-hubba—ha-ha-ha!*"

That night in the bright moonlight Musa brought bamboo sticks and mended the pen the foal had broken down. He put Hubba-Hubba and the Lame One inside it and wrapped himself in his blanket close by.

When he finally fell into a sleep, it was only to start up at a slight sound. "What are you up to now, tiny one?" he whispered.

This time it was Grandmother prowling around in the night. She was shoving her fine big gourd higher among the dried palm leaves on the rooftop. *"Hubba-hubba-hubba,"* he heard her muttering, but she broke off with a cry, "Musa, son, son! Did you hear?"

Musa was already on his feet and dragging the foal inside the house. The Lame One came stumbling in after. They shut the door fast. For they had heard a loud roar coming from somewhere close by. Ali's lion had come to life!

CHAPTER THREE

THE WHOLE VILLAGE crowded around the well the next morning, everyone telling his own part in the night's adventure.

"Yes," boasted the watchman, who had most certainly been asleep when the lion came over the wall of the pastureland. "I turned and there it was in the moonlight—the largest beast I have ever seen—making off with a plump young goat. But I got him. You will find the trail of blood leading off across the desert. He did not get far, you may be sure. And look!" He pointed to a group of vultures circling the air close by.

It had been many years since lions had troubled the village. Lions were like that. Sometimes they came in great bands, or again just a pair of them, now and then a lone one.

The old men told of days when the water hole out by the black rocks had been a favorite haunt for lions. But for years now the herdsmen had been sleeping out on the sand along-side their animals, depending on the small thornbush fires to scare off hyenas and wolves.

But now the lions were back. The village men knew that a wounded lion was the most dangerous of all, so all night long they had kept up a great din, beating drums, blowing horns, shouting, waving torches—anything to scare it away. Before dawn they were off to hunt it with guns and spears.

The goat girls and camel tenders drove their herds out, but kept them close to the village wall. Nor did they fold themselves in their robes, as they usually did, to sleep as soon as their charges started nibbling the scanty desert grass.

Grandmother took the Lame One and the foal out with her, saying she would keep an eye on them as she gathered red mullet leaves to make dye for her big gourd.

Musa did not sing that morning as he led the work camel up and down the path. He kept an anxious eye on the desert. But everything seemed as usual, and after a time quiet once more settled down over the little village. The only sound that could be heard was the creaking of the waterwheel and the voice of the weaver's wife, coaxing, "Speak, pretty one, speak. Say *Allah Akbar, Allah Akbar, Allah Akbar.*" Then abruptly she broke off with an angry, "*Hubba-hubba-hubba*—oh, you evil one!"

Musa dropped the camel rope and ran fast. Already there

was a crowd at her gate. And there stood the weaver's wife in the middle of her courtyard, her parrot's fine wicker cage a twisted mass at her feet. Worse still, the parrot was sitting free on top of the mud wall, crying, *"Hubba-hubba-hubba—ha-ha-ha!"*

Hubba-Hubba, the mischief maker, lay on his back kicking his feet high in the air and screaming with joy.

But the villagers were not in a mood for laughter this morning. They cried out loudly against the foal, "The runt should be destroyed!"

"How ever did the parrot get up there to the wall top?" one asked.

"Alas," the weaver's wife told them, "my husband went off with the other men to look for the lion this morning. I took the cage down to clean it. I left it on the ground for just one moment while I ran down the lane to get a fresh plantain leaf for it. Just one moment, alas, alas. . . ."

Hubba-Hubba struggled to his feet. He shook himself, stood with spindly legs splayed wide, blue stone dangling, nodding his head as though agreeing with every word she said. Crying out in rage, she reached for her bamboo stick and lunged toward him. But he shot past her, dodged Musa's hand, and disappeared down the lane with the parrot fluttering after him.

Now the weaver's wife wailed louder. And the women

tried to comfort her. "Never fear, the parrot will come back to his home after sundown. A bird raised from an egg fears to fly out into the world."

"Yes, and he had better come, for once the wild parrots catch the smell of man on him they will kill him."

At this moment the chief himself appeared. He clapped his hands to his ears. *"Wai, wai!* All this hubbub over a parrot! I thought it was a lion at least. You say your bird has flown, weaver's wife. Well," he glanced up into the trees, "the place is full of them. The pests spoil our noon sleep with their squawking. Any village boy can snare you another."

"But I have put in many long hours training this one to speak," the woman wailed. "It can say many words now. And look at my fine cage!"

The old man flung out his palms in disgust. "Why fuss over parrots and baskets when a lion prowls near our village?" He turned and spoke to the unhappy Musa, "Now I warned you before, water boy. You must go to find the parrot for the weaver's wife. Get her another cage too. If you don't," he pointed the long finger again, "I promise your foal will be sold as meat in the marketplace to pay for the loss."

Musa fled. As he passed the goat girl he cried out, "Which way did my camel go?"

"He just turned in your own gate. Run, run, Musa," she shouted back. Ameena had not taken her goats out to the desert

that morning because of the lion. They were now wandering happily through the villagers' vegetables.

Musa found Hubba-Hubba standing in the middle of the gourd patch. His eyes were shining at the sight of the red mullet leaves which Grandmother had just dumped on the ground. She was taking down her big gourd from the rooftop. *"Wai, wai, wai!"* she wailed. "See what that saucy bird has done, scratched it all up." She flapped the end of her scarf at the little gray parrot perched among the dried palm leaves. "Shoo, shoo, shoo!"

Musa darted forward crying, "No, no, no. Don't chase it away, Grandmother. That's the weaver's wife's parrot and Hubba-Hubba smashed . . ."

But at the word *hubba* the parrot broke out shrilly, *"Hubba-hubba-hubba-hubba—ha-ha-ha,"* and kept it up all the while Musa was telling what had happened. He ended with the chief's words, "And if I don't catch the parrot and get it back to her, get a cage too, my tiny camel will be sold in the marketplace for meat to pay for it."

The old woman stood fingering the gold coins at her neck, mumbling, *"Hankali, hankali.* Softly, softly, catch a monkey." It was an old village saying. Then she cried, "Go fast, son. Take your foal and keep him hidden till the thing is forgotten. I will catch the parrot for you."

Musa's heart was heavy as he led the foal, with the Lame

38

One limping behind, far off toward the black rocks, a part of the desert the villagers did not like.

Hubba-Hubba tugged hard against the rope at first, but grew quieter after a time. When he tired and tried to lie down, Musa forced him on. There was a real tussle when they came to the patch of purple camel-flower. Here he dropped down amid the green stems, kicked up his feet, and came up sneezing, covered with pollen. He looked hurt and puzzled at his master's cross tug.

Then they came to the water hole. It was the first time the foal had ever seen such a thing. He made a dash toward the lily pads and tall green reeds, squealing in terror as his pads went shooting out from under him in the slippery mud. He did not know that Allah had made his feet just for sand and rock. Musa dragged him up, a soggy little mass of muddy wool.

Another day Musa would have laughed, but today he groaned, "Alas, Hubba-Hubba, why can't you act like other foals?"

Then he pulled him fast from the water hole as a small bird down among the reeds let out a warning cry. It was the *a-bokin kada,* one the villagers called the friend of the crocodile. Even as it cried out, the long black snout on which it perched disappeared as if by magic into deep water.

There were footprints of many wild animals in the wet

mud and Musa's eyes widened in fear as he spotted some strange large ones—*a lion's.*

"Come, let us get out of here," he choked. And he turned aside into a thicket of old bamboo trees. Here the Lame One began to graze happily. But Hubba-Hubba, now loose, went dashing off only to come racing back a moment later, terrified by the sound of his own feet crunching on the hollow bamboo sticks. He lifted his nose high, listening. He huddled closer at the whistling of the wind in the green bamboo leaves above. He looked very little, very trusting. Musa went down on his knees and hugged him tight.

"No, no, no, they cannot take you from me," he cried. Now courage was rising again in his heart. He looked about him and suddenly his eyes lighted up. "A birdcage, a birdcage. I will *make* a birdcage!" And he quickly gathered up a pile of bamboo sticks. They were fine and dry, just in the right condition. He began to make another home for the parrot.

Using the knife he always carried at his waist, he slit the stalks into narrow pieces. He notched, fitted, and grooved. He tore the fiber from a nearby palm and used it to knot the bars fast together. He raised his eyes only to make sure the Lame One and her foal were still grazing nearby. More than once he had to stop to wipe blood from his fingers or draw a cruel splinter from them. The bamboo was hard to work with.

But bit by bit the cage began to take shape. First one side,

then another, another, another, then the bottom, then the top. It was late afternoon before he finally had it fitted together—a crude little box such as the villagers used for their doves in the marketplace. But to Musa, it was a fine piece of work, the cage which would save his foal's life.

He held it high now crying, "Oho, weaver's wife, here is your cage." But even as he spoke he remembered that there was still no parrot in it. And where was Hubba-Hubba? He jumped to his feet.

The Lame One was still grazing peacefully, but Hubba-Hubba was gone.

Now began a frantic search, through the thicket, down by the water hole, finally up toward the black rocks. The sun was low, a big red ball sinking into the sands; the village was a long way off. His voice filled the desert. "Hubba-Hubba-Hubba!"

He climbed at last on a high boulder, paused for breath and shouted the name again. "Hubba-Hubba!"

Then from right below came the answering squeal. He peered over. There lay the foal kicking pads in the air—and beside him, tapping playfully with huge fuzzy paws, was a golden-brown lion cub.

Musa swallowed hard. Not that he feared such a tiny cub as this. Its too-big head, its too-small legs told him it was but a few days old. With ease he could carry it away within his robe.

It would be many months before it became savage. No, he was not afraid of the cub. But a lion cub meant just one thing to him, a lion mother nearby. A lion father too, perhaps!

Musa came tumbling down over the rocks. In another moment he was tugging his foal back toward the bamboo grove. The lion cub still lay in the sand kicking up his paws.

It was almost dark when Musa came stumbling up the village lane. He was carrying the bamboo cage on his head and tugging the foal behind him. The Lame One was still out on the desert, limping in.

Musa dropped the cage inside his own gate as he passed, and shoved Hubba-Hubba's rope into Grandmother's hand. "A lion, I saw a lion," he gasped, and ran on.

"A lion! I saw a lion," he shouted to the crowd at the well.

"A lion! I saw a lion out there by the black rocks," he shouted again as he shoved past the guards at the chief's gate.

The old man was resting on a pile of leather cushions. He rose saying, "Slowly, boy, slowly. Many have seen lions by the black rocks in days gone by."

The villagers came crowding into the courtyard, remembering the goat that had been carried off in the night. Only Ali scoffed, "A fine tale. The mischievous camel and the missing parrot are forgotten when the lion prowls."

"Quiet!" the chief ordered. He turned to Musa, "Tell us what you saw out by the black rocks, water boy. How big was this lion?"

44

Musa stretched his arms the length of a lion cub. "Like this, and he rolled on the ground with my foal. . . ."

Now the people laughed again. And again the chief cried, "Quiet! Where was this, water boy?"

"Over beyond the pool where the crocodile lives. Beyond the bamboo groove."

"The haunt of the evil jinns? Why did you go there, boy?"

Musa looked downcast. "I went there to make a new cage for the weaver's wife." Then, suddenly bold when the villagers laughed loudly, he cried, "It is true! And you will find the chips I left out there."

"Yes," shouted Grandmother. She came through the crowd holding high a big bamboo cage. "And here it is. And the parrot inside it as well." She set it down before the chief.

"How did you catch the parrot?" asked Musa.

But now came the weaver's wife crying, "What! That ugly box my fine wicker cage with the scrolls on it? That scrawny little bird my pretty parrot? Never! *Wai, wai, wai!*"

There was a squeal from behind, and the crowd parted once more. In shot the tiny foal himself. He dashed up, rope trailing, and rose on his hind legs sniffing at the cage. He squealed again in joy, and from the cage came a shrill *"Hubba-hubba-hubba."* Everyone was laughing.

"There, weaver's wife, take your parrot," said the chief. He waved them aside as though tired of the affair. "The water

46

boy has done the best he could this day. You have your bird back and he will buy you another wicker cage as soon as he can get the silver coins. Off with you all now. We go to find that lion."

CHAPTER FOUR

Musa hurried his foal on down the lane. Ali had mocked at his story about the lion, but the chief had believed, and that was all that mattered. Now the drums were beating and the men were all running for their guns and spears. Already watchmen were taking their places by the mud wall.

The weaver's wife had gone off, muttering, with the despised bamboo cage.

Ali was back at his post at the well. He sat piping on a reed flute, the only thing he really liked to do. Musa, keeping his camel a safe distance from Ali's stick, called out, "Who leads the camel here at dawn? Do I?"

Ali feigned surprise, "You? Why I thought you had become a maker of birdcages." He shrugged, "No, the chief said

I was to tend the well tomorrow. And you were to tend that nuisance there."

Musa went on, dismayed for a moment. But when he looked at his camel his spirits rose. What could be better than to spend a whole day together?

He pulled Hubba-Hubba through the courtyard and back into the pen where the patient Lame One was waiting. He tied the foal fast, but stroked the soft nose comfortingly saying, "Alas, tiny one, you will have to have the rope till you learn to stay close to your mother."

Out in the courtyard now in the moonlight Grandmother was standing surrounded by the village women. She was telling how she had captured the weaver's wife's parrot. Until then no one had given her a chance.

"*Hankali, hankali.* Softly, softly, catch a monkey," Musa heard her repeating her favorite proverb as he came up. "After my poor grandson went off with such a sad face this morning, knowing that he was to lose his foal, I kept saying this, 'Softly, softly, catch a monkey.' For there sat that saucy parrot on my roof, rocking to and fro on the top of my gourd. You should just see that gourd. Wait only a minute." She hobbled up to get the gourd from the roof.

The women knew all about the fine gourd meant as a present for the chief. They had known about it from the day Grandmother had planted the seed, watered it with herbs, tied

50

its tiny green neck with vines to start its long narrow spout growing. Now here she was telling it again. "And the day I cut it I put it in a great bowl of water, left it there four days, which is the proper time. Then I cut off the head, scooped out the seeds, molded it into the proper shape, and set it up there on the roof to harden. Then . . ."

"Yes, yes, Grandmother," the women cried out. "But the parrot? How did you catch the parrot?"

Grandmother paused. "Yes, yes, I am coming to that. But first I must tell you about the gourd."

Some of the listeners clapped their hands to their heads. "The parrot, Grandmother? The parrot!"

"Yes, yes." The old woman's tone was sharp now. "But if there had been no gourd, there would have been no parrot in the cage this night. And my grandson's foal would now be . . ." Seeing Musa standing behind she broke off. "Yes, yes, now where was I?"

"The parrot, Grandmother."

"Ah, the parrot." She chuckled. "Well, this morning as I looked to see what harm he had done to my gourd I found a few seeds inside still. I took them out, flung them up to the mischief on the roof. But he was too sulky to eat. He just sat there, boring through me with those evil black eyes of his. But," she chuckled again, "I know parrots—and people. 'Softly, softly, catch a monkey,' I kept telling myself. So after he came flying

back—he had followed my grandson and the foal down the lane—I knew I had been right. He was not going to leave the thatch. But I got out my bag of fleece, sat there sorting it out, never so much as looking up toward him, but all the while watching him out of the corner of my eye.

"And after a time I saw him pecking around for those seeds I had tossed up. I got out a bowl of water, put it nearby, took down my gourd, rubbed it with oil." She held the gourd up again to show its glossy beauty. "Still I never looked toward him. He had come to the very edge of the roof, watching. I went into the house, and down he came for the water. He jumped on the edge of the gourd here, peered in, looking for more of those seeds. A wily bird that." She chuckled again. "But, as I have told my grandson, 'Softly, softly, catch a monkey.'"

"Go on, Grandmother, then what?"

"Yes, yes. The seeds. I had put aside a whole gourd of them to keep for planting next season. So I brought them out, dumped them into the gourd here, but leaving just one or two up here on this broad lip, see? I put the gourd back up in the thatch.

"Well, in no time at all, the greedy one had gobbled up the seeds on top, he was teetering round and round, beak poked down inside. My gourd was rocking so I feared it would come crashing down—"

"Throw your scarf, granny, throw your scarf over it now," one woman shouted, forgetting it was now over.

No one noticed her though, and Grandmother went on, enjoying her listeners. "No, no, no. *Hankali, hankali.* 'Softly, softly, catch a monkey,' I kept telling myself. And then suddenly, ha-ha-ha, down he went *inside.*"

Now there was great clapping of hands and jingling of bracelets and cries of "And then what? Then what?"

"Oho," Grandmother laughed at the memory. "There is an evil jinn inside that gourd now. Such a row, such squawking, such clawing inside that thing. My gourd comes rolling down through the thatch. At any moment it will crash. And finally it does."

"Alas, alas, your fine gourd!"

"No, no, here it is. I caught it. I tore off my scarf." She tugged off the faded cloth to show how she had done it. "I clap it down over the mouth of my gourd and take it fast into the house to await my grandson with the cage."

"But how did you know he would have it?" one called out.

"Of course he would have it. My grandson is his father's son. Do they lose a camel for a squawking bird?"

Musa went back to the pen. He lay down beside his two camels. He covered them with his blanket when the wind began to blow cold. Grandmother's words had made him brave for what might be on the morrow.

CHAPTER FIVE

The chief sent a messenger to Musa before dawn the next morning. "Take your place at the waterwheel," he said, "but see that you keep your foal tied fast in his pen today."

So the waterwheel was already turning when the hunters came riding in. The whole village crowded into the chief's courtyard after them.

They were tired and cross. "We hunted all night in the moonlight," they said. "We found no footprints by the pool but those of antelope, jackal, and hyena. We climbed the black rocks but found no lion. We found the sand all scattered nearby as if a small camel foal had been rolling in it, but no marks of a lion cub. We found a pile of bamboo chips over in the grove such as might be left by a youth whittling with a knife. . . ."

"The wind might have passed through, covering the marks

of the cub with sand," one began, but at this the weaver's wife appeared.

She was holding high the bamboo cage and shouting, "And this is not my parrot. Look at the ugly thing, hiding there in the corner. He does not eat. He does not speak. He is just some wild thing the water boy snared out there in the bamboo grove."

The chief spoke sternly, "You hear what the hunters say, boy. There is no lion. You hear what the weaver's wife says. This is not her bird. You know the punishment for lying in this village. Very well," he turned to his guards, "take the boy and beat him well."

But before the guards could move forward, Ameena came running in crying, "A caravan, a caravan is coming! I have just seen it on the desert."

And now everyone joined in the cry. The arrival of a caravan was a great event in the little village. Musa was forgotten as the villagers rushed around getting ready to trade their wares.

The chief put on his best embroidered robe and beaded cap. He sent two men to the well, one to lead the camel and one with a basket to hold the cowrie shells with which the travelers would pay for water. The villagers had their water free, but strangers had to give a handful of the gray cowrie shells for each bucket emptied into trough or goatskin flask.

Down in the marketplace the women were already piling

fruits and vegetables and trinkets on their mats. The blacksmith appeared with an armful of spears and knives in leather sheaths. The camel trader sent his son Ali to bring in all the herds fast, since newcomers might be thieves.

The weaver's wife shoved her despised birdcage on the wall out of the way, and helped her husband unroll his pieces of fine camel-wool cloth. Grandmother gave her gourd a rub with oil and set it carefully up on the roof.

Musa, finding there was no place for him at the well, made his way into the date-palm grove. Here the women were hurriedly packing big plump dates which the grower had just cut that morning. He was saying, "What luck! The palm trees bear but one cluster a year, and here today I have a dozen fine juicy clusters hanging ready."

He also brought out baskets of old dates dried hard as stone, the dates the desert men live on when far from an oasis. Dates that would be used for soup for weary or nursing camels. Date pits that would be ground up to make meal for goats.

But now the caravan was drawing near. They came in chanting as desert men always do when the well lies just ahead. They shouted, *"Allah Akbar, Allah Akbar!"* as they halted outside the village down toward the black rocks.

It was only a small group, some fifty camels loaded with salt and goatskins and big bags of camel's hair. They did not un-

load or start to put up their black tent until the headman had ridden across to bargain for water.

The chief's servant rode out to meet the stranger, a fierce-looking man in a dark blue robe and cloth wound high around his head, the end brought across his face against wind and sun. He carried a knife in his belt, a gun in his hand.

The two men bowed low before each other. The stranger said, "We are honorable men from the salt-mine village far in the desert. We have been journeying many days. We carry goat-skins and salt to Kano market, seven days' journey ahead. We would trade some of our salt for your fresh dates and water."

"Alas," the chief's man flung his palms out, "Our well is nearly dry. We have scarcely enough for our own herds. How would we fill the goatskins for fifty men, let alone fill the bellies of fifty thirsty animals coming in from the hot sands? I fear we would have to charge you ten handfuls of cowrie shells for each bucket of water."

"Ten handfuls a bucket! *Wai, wai, wai,*" he wailed. "Why, we have been filling our waterskins all across the desert and never had to pay more than a half-handful for a bucket."

Now the villagers all gathered around to take part in the argument which always followed at this point. Their shouts rose so high it seemed as though war was about to break out.

But finally the two headmen settled for the usual price—

a handful of cowries for a bucket of water. They bowed low and went off smiling.

For the next hour all was confusion in the village. The creak of the waterwheel rose high above the roars and spitting of the camels at the trough. "No, no, no," the chief's man kept shouting. He stayed the bucket that would have dumped its contents into the goatskins. "Cowries first, then water." The strangers swore as they dug deep into their bags of shells.

The villagers waited impatiently all this while. The caravan was moving on the next day, and much trading would have to be done that night. Salt was the one thing they all wanted. Salt was as necessary as water to men and animals on the desert. And salt was low now.

They crowded around as the strangers came in with buckets of salt chopped from the big dirty gray slabs they were carrying across the desert.

"A good thing I had my beads all ready," said one villager. "I sat up late only last night blowing glass through that reed, making those fine colored ones that the women wear around their hips. Such beads they do not find in Kano markets."

"And I made mine from the shell of an ostrich egg mixed with flour. Hard as rock and with patterns such as they do not see in Kano either," said another.

The leather worker held up a very fine saddle, tooled in a

fancy design and with great iron stirrups dangling from it. "And I am sure there is no saddle in Kano like this. How many buckets of salt do you think he will give for this?"

The crowd followed the strangers through the lanes, taking part in all the trading. They clapped hands to heads and wailed at the hard bargains the newcomers were driving.

The headman traded at first for a few goats, a few baskets of dates. He shook his head when people began to bring out the big loose sacks of camel's hair they had been gathering now for months. "No, no, no," he cried, "we have as much fleece now as we can carry." But they all knew that fleece was really what he wanted most.

The headman was moving from gate to gate with the villagers following behind. Ali, the camel trader's son, had a saucy word at each stop. "Oho!" he cried out as they came to Musa's house. "There is a fine big gourd for you up on the rooftop, headman."

"Why would I carry a gourd to Kano?" the headman said, and all laughed.

But Grandmother was calling out eagerly, "No, wait, wait!" She hastened into the house and dragged out a great sack of white fleece. "See, headman, fleece from one of royal blood, the fastest camel of our village, fed on date-pip soup, coat combed every day. See, it is like silk. It is used only for the scarves of kings."

64

The headman pulled out a handful, felt it, tossed it in the air. "How much, Grandmother?" he asked.

"Five silver coins," she spoke quickly.

"To pay the weaver's wife for her parrot," Ali shouted.

The headman laughed. "What have you got hidden in the sack, old woman, gold? Five buckets of salt for the fleece."

But just then they heard a sound of splintering wood from the back of the house. Hubba-Hubba came sprinting around the corner, trailing a broken rope. He sniffed at the fleece on the ground and went sprawling into it. He scrambled up, shook himself and sneezed, rose on hind legs, and began to dance round and round squealing with joy. And from the bamboo cage on the wall came a cry of *"Hubba-hubba-hubba-hubba, Allah Akbar, Allah Akbar"* which brought the weaver's wife shouting, "My parrot, my pretty one, he speaks, he speaks!"

Everyone was laughing. The headman poked his finger into Hubba-Hubba's tiny hump and said, "How much for this runt?"

"Yes, he will make tender meat," cried Ali.

"No, no," the man shook his head. He did not see the terror on Grandmother's face. "I don't want him for meat. He's a clown. A dancing clown. I know a man in Kano who is looking for just such a foal to train for his traveling fair."

Ali, who longed above all to see Kano, pressed in closer. One of the villagers was saying, "Yes, I've seen those traveling fairs. There was one with a big bear that danced. And a monkey dressed as a white man, with a sun hat."

"But those camels don't dance for joy," a woman cried sharply. "I have been told they are put in a bamboo cage, and

they dance from pain because a fire burns beneath the iron plates on which they stand."

But the headman was growing more eager. "Yes," he said, "I will give you five silver coins for the foal, old woman. And," he glanced toward the cage on the wall, "another for the parrot up there. They go well together."

Without waiting to hear more, Musa seized his pet and dragged him out of sight.

CHAPTER SIX

THEY WENT FAR OUT across the desert to a spot well away from the black tent. Musa tied Hubba-Hubba fast to a thornbush, then sat hugging his knees, staring unhappily across the sands. He could see Ameena following her goats. Closer—and now Musa's face clouded—there was Ali bringing his father's herd out. "And for shearing," he told himself as he saw the men forcing the animals to kneel, tying their feet, women at their heads.

Usually the people in this small village did no shearing. Camels shed their hair all year long, but faster as the hot season drew near till at last the creatures were quite naked-looking. Women spent days out gathering the big wads of matted wool from sand or thornbush. It was not yet the hot season, and the camels were all still wearing their heavy coats. But Ali's father, anxious to trade, had decided to fill his sacks by shearing.

Musa watched Ali riding up and down on his pony, urging the shearers on. He watched as the mounds of brown wool rose higher and the women stuffed it into the sacks that were to carry it on to Kano. He watched the caravan, too. Off toward the black rocks the men were loading up for the journey.

But to Musa, used to moving up and down the path from the well, the day seemed long. The Lame One had finished grazing and was now sleeping, her neck stretched out on the hot sand as though in bliss.

Hubba-Hubba, who had gamboled about for a time not seeming to mind the rope, lay some distance from his mother in exactly the same position, asleep.

Musa drew his scarf over his face, edged in under the thornbush, and closed his eyes too.

He wakened with a start—Hubba-Hubba was gone! And the Lame One was up staring anxiously across the sand. Had the foal run away again—or had he been stolen?

Musa scrambled to his feet. There were fresh hoof marks in the sand leading right past the thornbush where part of the tiny one's rope still hung. The tiny pads had skipped, circled as they always did, then shot off across the desert toward the village.

Musa ran to the group of camel shearers with the Lame One limping painfully after him. The men were just putting away their great sharp shears as the camels struggled to their feet. The women were hastily stuffing the last of the wool into the big sacks, a cloud of gold rising in the air.

"Has anyone here seen my foal, Hubba-Hubba?" Musa yelled, trying to make himself heard above the roar of the noisy animals.

"Yes," a man's voice came back, "and I took my stick to the saucy runt. He started the whole herd up. I warn you, water boy, if you don't keep that thing of yours out of the way, someone is going to kill him one day."

"But where did he go?" begged Musa.

A woman tying up a sack nearby, seeing his face, took pity and said, "No, no, Musa, he just talks that way. He chased the foal but did not bring his stick down on that tiny hump. Someone caught him and sent him on over to your grandmother."

Musa went running on to the village. He reached his own courtyard hoping somehow to see that little white figure with the blue stone dangling at his neck waiting for him. But there was only Grandmother. And she was huddled in the doorway, shawl drawn over her face, silent.

"Hubba-Hubba? My tiny one?" he cried out in terror.

She raised her head then, and he saw she had been weeping a long time. She said dully, "The fleece is gone. So too your little camel."

"Yes," it was the weaver's wife calling over the wall, "and my pretty parrot. Gone, gone, gone, all gone." She pulled her scarf over her face and began to wail loudly.

Musa stared from one to the other. "You sold your parrot? And you, Grandmother . . ." he looked shocked.

"No, no, silly one." The weaver's wife dried her tears and told the story. "They were stolen. And by that evil-eyed headman. They are all villains who come from those salt mines out on the desert. I knew the minute I looked at him."

"Who else could it be?" The woman's voice grew shriller. "He came here followed by the crowd of urchins and that Ali who should have been out tending his father's camels. But do you think he came for your grandmother's gourd? Or do you think he cared when he saw how fat she had made that sack of fine white fleece? No. All he wanted was my parrot and that Hubba-Hubba of yours. 'Where's the foal?' he kept shouting. 'I'll give you ten silver coins for him. And ten silver coins for the parrot.' And every time my poor parrot cried *"Hubba-hubba-hubba"* up on the wall top the man offered still more coins. He went off in a great rage at last, taking with him only the sack of fleece. Or so was thought. . . ." She spoke bitterly now. "Till we came out a little later and found parrot and foal both gone."

"Is this so, Grandmother?" Musa asked.

But at his gentle tone she covered her face again and began to weep. Musa looked over at the weaver's wife. "Have you looked well for them?"

"Yes, we have looked well."

And Musa with fear mounting high in his heart now turned back to the desert.

He stood then for a long time, straining his eyes toward any small white object in the distance. The desert, usually sleeping at this time of day, was all astir. Men and camels were moving in and out from the caravan, carrying big sacks and goatskins of water. And coming in close to him was Ameena with her flock of goats.

She was running now, skirts and pigtails flying, her brown arms waving excitedly. "Musa, Musa, I have something to tell you," she cried. "It's about Hubba-Hubba." She was struggling for breath now. "I know where he is."

He seized her arm, demanding, "Where, where?"

"Over there in the black tent." She pointed off across the desert to the caravan. "My father traded three goats for a bucket of salt and he sent a boy out to me to tell me to drive them over there to the caravan. They are making haste, he said, because they move on tonight."

"But Hubba-Hubba?"

"I am coming to that, Musa. I drove my three goats across there, leaving the others to wander where they would. They ran all ways, the three I mean, when I got them over there.

In and out between the baskets and the sacks. And there was no one at the black tent to take the goats from me. They were all in the village still trading salt, I suppose."

"Yes, yes, Ameena . . ." he was frantic now, waiting for the rest of the story.

Her eyes grew big and her voice sank to a whisper. "So I went wandering around to find someone, and what do you think I heard?"

"What?"

"*Hubba-hubba-hubba*—that's what I heard. And it was the weaver's parrot crying it."

"And where was he?"

"Inside that big black tent, Musa."

"But Hubba-Hubba . . ."

"Then I heard Hubba-Hubba give that silly little squeal as he does when he has done something wrong. . . ."

Musa did not wait to hear more. He was off across the desert, scarf flying, shabby robe flapping around his thin brown legs. He was heading fast for that black tent.

CHAPTER SEVEN

Musa pushed in among the crowd of village youths watching the caravan load. There were always envious eyes on such a day. However, Ali, who wanted to go to Kano more than any of the youths, was not there.

There was much dust and noise. The camels spit and bared teeth as they lumbered down to their knees. The drivers shouted at the youths to get out of the way. They cursed the ropes that would not knot around unwieldly salt baskets and sacks. It was easy to slip away unnoticed.

Musa crept cautiously in between the many baskets and bundles and came close to the black goatskin tent. Inside he thought he heard a labored breathing as of one tugging. Then came a squeal. Musa went down flat and squirmed under the rug over the door.

Inside all was dark and musty. Gradually he made out the piles of saddles, sacks, yes—he peered closer—a bamboo cage upturned, a basket of dates trampled in the sand, and Hubba-Hubba shaking himself free from a sack of white fleece.

The foal was standing, matted with date and fleece even to his eyelashes, straddling the mess he had made. He sneezed. Unable to see, he began to stumble around, squealing pitifully. And from the upturned cage came *"Hubba-hubba-hubba—ha-ha-ha!"*

An angry voice outside shouted, "What's going on in there?" Musa crouched low behind a sack.

The flap shot up letting in a flood of light, and in strode the headman. He clapped his hands to his head, groaning, "Alas, alas, my basket of dates. And my fleece—why, you evil little runt!" Musa, peeping out from his hiding place, closed his eyes as he saw the man grab a stick and lunge toward Hubba-Hubba.

The foal dodged this way and that. He stumbled over the birdcage. He found the door and went tearing out, with the headman shouting after him, "Catch him, catch the foal!"

Down at Musa's feet there was a faint cluck. He grabbed the birdcage and ran after his foal, racing across the sands. When Hubba-Hubba neared the black rocks, he disappeared into a patch of camel-flowers.

Musa came after, robe flapping about his thin legs, the birdcage still in his arms. He paused at a lone acacia tree to

shove the cage far in among the leaves and yellow flowers, and glanced around. There was no one following. Nor could he hear any longer the headman's voice crying, "Stop him, stop him, stop him!"

He ran on now to the spot where he thought he had last seen his foal. But Hubba-Hubba had chosen a fine hiding place. The camel-flower grew thick and waist-high. It spread like a great purple blanket on the sand, unrippled by the slightest wind.

Musa stood mopping his face with the end of his scarf, his eyes searching the patch. "Hubba-Hubba!" he called. But there was no answering squeal, and his fear was growing as he shoved through the thick flowers. Had the headman's blows been too much? Or had some wild animal pounced on his foal?

He looked back toward the caravan. The camels stood, loaded now, a long black line against the setting sun, tied nose-to-tail. Even as he looked, the big black tent went flopping down like a cut mushroom.

He looked beyond toward the waterhole. Soon the hyenas and jackals—yes, and perhaps the lions—would come to drink.

He looked toward the village. But oh, what a long way off it was! In the sky above him three great vultures were circling. "Hubba-Hubba, Hubba-Hubba!" he let out a wild shout.

80

And now a small white nose shot up through the purple flowers. "Hubba-Hubba," Musa was fairly sobbing. He pushed through the flowers, falling on his knees and gathering the foal close in his arms.

Then he drew away to see what harm had been done to him. Had it been any other time Musa would have laughed. And could the villagers have seen Hubba-Hubba at that moment, they would surely have taken him for one of the evil jinns that haunted the desert.

Hubba-Hubba was plastered thick from head to toe with dates, fleece, pollen, and purple petals. His long lashes were glued fast together. Torn sacking still clung to the rope at his neck.

"Alas, tiny one, you are blind." Musa looked back toward the desert. The caravan stood loaded as it had some minutes ago. It might be there for hours. He glanced toward the water hole again. The sun was going down rapidly now, but something had to be done for the unhappy foal.

So he led him down to the water-hole, keeping a firm grip as they went through the slippery mud. They drank long at the warm muddy water, then he dipped his scarf and washed off the tiny nose. The foal would have stayed, dabbling, but Musa said, "No, no. We will have to wait till that caravan moves out before we clean up the rest of you."

They went back to the safety of the camel-flowers.

That night the wind blew cold across the desert. But Musa and his camel slept soundly close together in the camel-flowers, covered with Musa's robe. They were both worn out from their terrible day.

At dawn Musa pulled himself up and looked around wide-eyed at the purple flowers and green bamboo. He was shivering. He rubbed his eyes, saw the little hollow beside him; then he remembered and got quickly to his feet. Where was Hubba-Hubba? Gone again.

He knotted his sash about him, looking fearfully across the desert. The caravan had gone. There stood the lone acacia tree outlined now against the sky. "Poor parrot," he thought. But worse still, "Poor little Hubba-Hubba."

He pushed through the camel-flowers, found the tiny foal's marks, and tracked them to the waterhole. He stopped by a pile of freshly picked bones. The vultures perched close by watching him. But they were not camel bones, and he hastened on calling the foal by name, "Hubba-Hubba, Hubba-Hubba!"

The footprints led on now past the bamboo grove where the morning mist still hung heavy, on past the pile of shavings he had left from his birdcage, on up toward the black rocks. His heart was thumping as he neared them.

The villagers had laughed at his story of the lion. Ali had called him a liar. But Musa himself knew the truth. He knew

82

too that this was the hour of the day when the lion came home to sleep after preying on the village goats. Was he there now?

Musa crept to the spot where two nights before he had found Hubba-Hubba playing with the cub. There was no sight of them now, but—had he heard a purr?

He cast a frightened glance toward the wall of rock behind, then edged closer and looked over into the hollow from where the sound was coming.

There just below him were the two young ones playing as before, Hubba-Hubba on his back, hair matted thick with dirt, the lion cub catching at the bit of torn sacking still tangled in the foal's rope.

Musa's eyes flashed to the rock above. Then he saw the lion. She was rising slowly into crouching position, looking down at the two on the ground. Hubba-Hubba's pad shot out catching the cub too hard, and as it let out a whimper, her ugly lips began to curl back. She rose a little higher.

Now Musa was staring into two blazing golden eyes. He stood as one in a spell. The lion's ruff of hair was bristling. There was a low rumble which Musa knew came just before the roar, the leap.

His eyes were still held fast by those blazing golden ones, but his fingers were groping for something, anything. They closed on a sharp piece of rock. Then, at a sudden twitching

of the lion's great body, he let fly. The rock struck the lion straight between the eyes. And to Musa's surprise the huge beast crumpled and was still.

Musa stood, too terrified to run. The two small ones were still rolling on the sand.

The lion lay quiet. Dead, Musa thought. But no, that could not be. Not by a bit of rock. No, no, he knew these beasts of the desert. They were full of tricks. In another instant this one would be up, springing out at him, at Hubba-Hubba.

But the minutes passed and he stood still, unable to pull himself away, and the lion up on the rock was lying, eyes closed, rigid. He began to feel he had indeed killed it. He tossed another small stone.

He crept a little closer, peering hard. He picked up a stick, poked at the big paw hanging limp over the edge. Still no move. He pulled himself up on the ledge, touched another of those huge furry paws. It was still warm, but the lion was dead.

Dropping to the ground, Musa ran to get his foal. He found the end of Hubba-Hubba's rope and pulled his camel from the spot.

He had gone only a few steps, however, when he heard a whimper. Turning, he saw the cub waddling fast after him. Hubba-Hubba let out a squeal and tugged on the rope. Musa stopped, troubled. He glanced back toward the cave. The tiny thing's mother lay still, just as he had left her.

He took the cub in his arms, and still holding fast to Hubba-Hubba's rope, he started for the village.

CHAPTER EIGHT

As Musa stumbled across the sand clutching the lion cub close and dragging the wilful camel after him, he was still trembling with fear. "The lion is dead, the lion is dead," he kept telling himself. But at any moment he expected to hear a great roar behind him.

He shoved through the camel-flowers, and here Hubba-Hubba was a terrible nuisance. He was determined to lie down, to rest among the green leaves as he had in the night. The cub sleeping peacefully in Musa's arms was a heavy weight.

When he came to the one acacia tree, Musa paused to rest, also to peer back among the branches. The parrot was still there perched safely in his cage, and now the beady eye was fixed on the little brown creature in Musa's arms.

As Musa started to leave, the parrot began to scream

"*Hubba-hubba-hubba!*" And Hubba-Hubba, planting his feet firmly in the sand, refused to budge. Musa stood looking unhappily about him. Of one thing he was certain: if he had to leave one of these three behind, it would not be his foal.

Then his face brightened as he saw a band of villagers galloping toward him, some on camel, others on pony.

"So here you are, water boy." They sounded cross. "Here we are out searching the desert for you, thinking the vultures had picked your bones clean by this time."

"Or else you had been carried off by that thieving caravan lot."

"And your grandmother wailing all night for you as one dead!"

"But what have you there?" one asked. "Oho! A lion cub!"

Musa was suddenly very bold. He held the cub up for all to see. "I bring a pet home for our chief." Then, as they crowded close crying out in surprise, he said, "And I killed the lion."

"You killed the lion!"

Musa waved back toward the black rocks. "And if you looked, you would see it lying there among the rocks right now.

"And," he went on, "I bring back the parrot in his cage which I made for the weaver's wife. You will find him safe in this tree." To their surprise, when one of them reached in, he did bring out the bamboo cage with the parrot unharmed but ruffling his feathers crossly.

"And I bring back my tiny camel, which will one day be

88

the fastest runner on all the desert!" At that very moment Hubba-Hubba saw his mother, who was following behind the villagers. Having not had a proper drink of milk for many hours, he pulled loose and went racing to her.

"*Wai, wai, wai,*" the men were all murmuring admiringly. "How did you do it, water boy?"

"Would I let that thief from the caravan carry off my foal? Or the weaver's wife's parrot?"

"Ah, but the headman was not the thief," one explained "It was Ali, the camel trader's son. The headman came running to the village to tell how the foal and parrot he had bought to sell to the circus in Kano had been stolen from him. And when he spotted Ali lurking behind the wall, he cried, 'Oho! there's the youth who took my money. Now let him go bring me back the foal and bird!' "

"And where is Ali now?" Musa had forgotten to be boastful hearing this news.

"Who knows? Perhaps he is hiding deep in one of the salt baskets on his way to Kano. Never fear, he will pay for his deeds."

And now the hunters on horseback went off to see the lion. And Musa was lifted on a camel, still holding his cub close in his arms. The parrot in its bamboo cage was taken by another.

So they came riding into the village, up through the narrow lane, stopping at the chief's gate where Musa went in and put the lion cub down before him.

"I have brought you a lion to train as your guard, O Chief," he said. For this was thought to be the finest gift one could give a chief.

And the chief said, "I now appoint you as my lion trainer, water boy—appoint you too to train that foal of yours," for at that moment Grandmother had appeared holding the dirty little Hubba-Hubba.

Now Musa told all that had happened to him. Everyone in the village cried, "*Wai, wai,* he is brave, the water boy! What courage!" Even the weaver's wife was happy.

In fact, no one listened as the men came riding in from the desert shouting, "But it was the watchman's shot that really killed the lion. She was in her last agony when Musa's stone struck her." No, everyone went on saying, "Musa killed the lion. What a brave boy!"

And Musa, tugging his tiny camel after him, went down the lane singing his father's song:

Swift as a bird my camel speeds,
Nor wind, nor sand, nor lion heeds.
Round his neck a blue stone charm
To keep him safely from all harm. . . .

GLOSSARY

A-BOKIN KADA—friend of the crocodile. This small bird sits on the crocodile's head and alerts him to danger.

ALLAH AKBAR—"God is Victorious." Phrase heard every day in Equatorial Africa. It is the cry used by caravans when reaching a well and is also a battle cry of victory. .

AMEENA—name of an ancient, powerful, Hausa queen. This is perhaps the most popular name for girls in West Africa.

COWRIE SHELLS—small, gray snail shells found in the Indian Ocean. They are used as money all over North and Equatorial Africa, and are worth about 1/16th of a penny. In payment they are counted by handfuls, or used in sacks of 1,000 to 100,000. Women wear them around their necks in strings of 40 to 100 to show their wealth.

G-R-R-R—sound used to make a camel run.

HANKALI—softly. As in "hubba-hubba," the word is often used twice.

HAUSAS—one of several tribes living in and beyond the Niger land, formerly Colonial West Africa. The people are dark skinned and noted for spinning, weaving, and dyeing. Hausa villages differ in customs and dress, but they are united by the same tongue. Hausa is the language spoken by traders from the West Coast across the Sahara to the Nile and as far north as Tunis and Alexandria. It is understood by most Africans in that area, more so than is English or French.

HUBBA—trouble or mischief. The double form of hubba-hubba is used commonly in Africa.

ICKTH ICKTH—sounds used to make a camel kneel.

JINNS—spirits which desert men believe infest the desert, particularly peaks and valleys. They are sometimes evil, sometimes good.

KANO—large city in Northern Nigeria, one of the oldest and still largest caravan markets in the country. It is also a great international airport today.

LAME ONE—name given to the camel Racer when it became old. Animals are never given names of human beings, but rather the names of virtues or faults.

MUSA—a very popular name for boys in the Sahara and West Africa. It comes from Moses and is pronounced "Moó-sa."

SAHARA—desert region extending from the Atlantic coast of Africa to the Red Sea. The word means abundance.

SOFTLY, SOFTLY, CATCH A MONKEY—well-known proverb in this part of Africa. It means to move carefully when after a wily one.

Expressions like "Allah preserve us!" are used so commonly that they have become a form of slang.